Be Kind, Francis the Fly

To Zoe & Nick,

Enjoy learning
with Frances! I loved
creating him on paper.
Your friend at MST.

Love, Pat
Miss Pat
Pat Clark
4-4-09

Be Kind, Francis the Fly

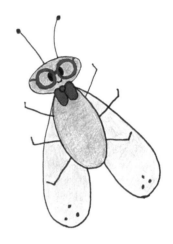

By
Karen R. Weaver
Illustrated by Pat Clark

Mill City Press
Minneapolis, MN

Mill City Press, Inc.
212 3rd Avenue North, Suite 570
Minneapolis, MN 55401
612.455.2294
www.millcitypublishing.com

ISBN - 978-1-934937-50-1
ISBN - 1-934937-50-9
LCCN - 2008942208

Cover Design and Typeset by Sophie Chi

Printed in the United States of America

In loving memory of my brother,
Father James Francis Edmiston
July 18, 1954 - May 18, 2008.

Galatians 5:22-23 *"But the fruit of the
Spirit is love, joy, peace, patience,
kindness, goodness, faithfulness,
gentleness and self control. Against
such things there is no law."* (NIV)

Friar Jim was walking through the meadow enjoying all the beautiful flowers and bugs. His friend, Francis the fly was playing among the flowers.

Francis got bored, so he started buzzing around Friar Jim's head. BZZZZZ......

Friar Jim gently waved his hand at Francis and added, "Shoo, Shoo! You are being a pest and need to stop. You need to be kind."

Francis said, "What does kind mean?" Friar Jim sat down in the middle of the meadow and told Francis a story about his friend Brian.

Brian loved to play at the park
with his dog Fur Ball.

Fur Ball sat and watched Brian
go down the slide really fast.

After Brian played on the slide, he started playing frisbee with Fur Ball but it was hot and they got very tired and thirsty.

It was a good thing Brian's mom had some water for them. He sat in the shade and drank his water, and shared some with Fur Ball.

After Brian finished his water, he ran over to the swings and left Fur Ball sitting in the shade to rest. Brian tried very hard to make the swing go, but he just couldn't do it.

Kaylee, a little girl playing nearby, noticed that Brian had stopped trying. He seemed very sad. She stopped playing with her ball and asked him, "What's wrong?"

Brian replied, "I can't swing!"
"I can help you," she said. "I'll push and you move your legs back and forth."
He went very, very high. Fur Ball barked with glee as he watched. "Ruff, Ruff"

Brian was so happy that he was swinging so high. He said, "Thank you for helping me swing. You are so kind!" Kaylee replied, "You're welcome."

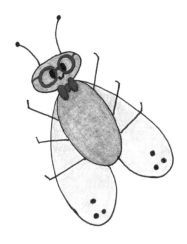 

Friar Jim told Francis, "Kaylee was being kind to Brian. She was being a good friend. Kaylee cared that he was sad and wanted to make him happy again so, she stopped playing with her ball and helped Brian swing."

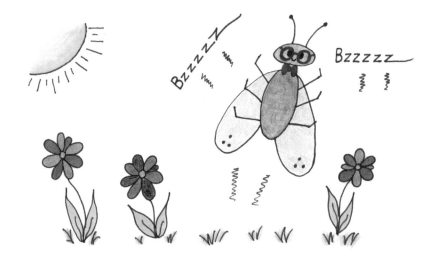

Francis buzzed around the flowers happily and said, "I don't want to be a pest and fly around your head. I want to be kind too." BZZZZZ! "What can I do to help?" BZZZZZ!

Karen Weaver resides in Northern Virginia with her husband. She has two children and one grandchild. For the past 16 years she has been working with children ages 2-6 as either a preschool teacher or Daisy Girl Scout Leader. When not working with children, she enjoys knitting and working puzzles.

Printed in the United States
136947LV00001B